ABOUT OUR TALE

For our retelling of this tale, we mainly drew inspiration from two Greek versions. The story line is roughly based on our translation of the orphan's tale told by Daskalaki, as found in Chatzitaki-Kapsomenou's *The Modern Greek Folktale,* from which we also took our title. From our translation of Loukatos's version of the tale in *Modern Greek Folk Texts,* we borrowed and elaborated on the passing reference to religious themes, and we also found the image of the honey and decided to make it a vital plot device.

We decided to give our heroine the option to step out of the traditional role in which she waits patiently for her prince. Many of the Greek Cinderellas we met stayed in their place at home—in the ashes, in dark corners, in storerooms—submissive to their destiny as women and unable to take the initiative to decide their fate. Unlike these characters, our orphan emerges as a self-determined young woman who takes it upon herself to go and find her prince.

Text copyright © 2011 by Anthony L. Manna and Christodoula Mitakidou
Illustrations copyright © 2011 by Giselle Potter
All rights reserved. Published in the United States by
Schwartz & Wade Books, an imprint of Random House Children's Books,
a division of Random House, Inc., New York.
Schwartz & Wade Books and the colophon
are trademarks of Random House, Inc.

Library of Congress Cataloging-in-Publication Data
is available upon request.
ISBN 978-0-375-86691-3 (trade) — ISBN 978-0-375-96691-0 (glb)
— ISBN 978-0-375-98500-3 (ebook)
MANUFACTURED IN CHINA
10 9 8 7 6 5 4 3 2 1
First Edition

The Orphan

A Cinderella Story from Greece

by Anthony L. Manna & Soula Mitakidou

illustrated by Giselle Potter

schwartz & wade books · new york

One time in a time in Greece there lived a mother, a father, and their daughter. Never had a girl been cared for with such tenderness. The mother tended to her every need, bathing her in musk-scented water, combing her long, dark hair with an ivory comb, and singing her to sleep in a bed of down.

When the girl was still young, cruel fate took the mother's
life and left the poor child an orphan, for as people say in Greece,
"A child becomes an orphan when she loses her mother."

The orphan's father soon took a new wife, a cruel woman who had two spoiled daughters. Upon her own girls the woman lavished countless treasures. Upon the orphan, she lavished nothing but grief. So hateful was she that she counted every drop of water the orphan was allowed to drink!

One night, the poor orphan fled to her mother's grave. Throwing herself on the ground, she cried:

"Oh, Mother, dear Mother,
Listen to my plea!
A stranger tries to take your place,
But does not care for me.
Her daughters call me 'sister' now,
But are heartless as can be.
Oh, Mother, dear Mother,
I beg you, set me free!"

At once, the grave trembled, and the mother's voice rose from the earth:

"Go, my child, go to good,
With all my blessings, go!
Your sorrow weighs upon my heart,
Your pain, it wounds me so.
Go, my child, go to good,
Don't cry and don't despair.
Go home, my soul, and wait to find
True fortune's blessings there."

And so, holding close her mother's words,
the orphan followed the moon's path home.

The next day, as darkness dissolved, the orphan stepped outside to begin her chores. At once, Mother Nature and her children appeared in all their glory and showered her with gifts. The Sun gave her brilliance; the Moon, beauty; the Dawn bestowed gracefulness. And that was not all—the Morning Star let her wear the Evening Star as a wreath; the Meadows gave her three beautiful dresses, and the Sea, a pair of delicate blue shoes to fit her tiny feet.

After thanking them all, the orphan rushed inside and hid her treasures in a trunk.

Now, it so happened that the prince of the kingdom decided to attend the service at the village's church that very Sunday.

"Imagine!" declared the orphan's stepmother upon hearing the news. "If the prince is clear-eyed enough to be enraptured by my girls' beauty, he is sure to choose one for his bride." And at once she demanded that her husband hire the village's best tailors to make lavish gowns for herself and her two daughters.

What did the father do?

What *could* he do?

Why, he hired the village's best tailors to make three gowns, of course— one of brocade, one of damask, and one of pure silk.

But still the stepmother was not satisfied. Now she used her charm to convince her husband that she and the girls also needed fine jewels to wear.

What did the father do?

What *could* he do?

Yes, he bought his wife a necklace of sapphires, one daughter a bracelet of red rubies, and the other a gleaming gold ring set with garnets.

Come Sunday, as darkness dissolved, the stepmother ordered the orphan to fix her stepsisters' hair in the most elaborate styles of the day and dress them in the lavish new gowns.

Then, like royalty, the
girls and their mother paraded
through the village.

Once inside the church,
they sashayed down the aisle
and took their place close to the
altar, where a throne awaited the
prince's arrival.

Meanwhile, as soon as the orphan was alone, her mother's words came to her.

"Go, my child, go to good,
With all my blessings, go!
Your sorrow weighs upon my heart,
Your pain, it wounds me so.
Go, my child, go to good,
Don't cry and don't despair.
Go home, my soul, and wait to find
True fortune's blessings there."

Quickly, the orphan opened the trunk and pulled out Mother Nature's gifts. At the very bottom, she was surprised to find piles upon piles of gold coins.

As her mother had once done for her, the orphan bathed herself in musk-scented water and combed her hair with an ivory comb. Then she put on her gown stitched with flowers of the meadow, her wreath of the Evening Star, and her tiny shoes the color of the deep blue sea.

Instantly, she became as brilliant as the sun, as beautiful as the moon, as graceful as the dawn. She dropped a handful of coins into her pocket. Then she stepped outside.

Raising her hands, the orphan reached to the sky. And like that, a cloud fell at her feet and turned into a radiant white mare. The orphan mounted it and set off, as quick as the wind, for the village church.

Along the way, her mother's voice spoke to her again, rustling through the trees:

"You must remember, my soul,
to return home the minute the service ends,
or all will be lost."

The orphan leapt from the mare and ran
inside the church. Making her way down the
aisle, she looked neither right nor left, but only
toward the altar, where the prince now sat.

All eyes followed the beautiful stranger's every move. Remembering later, a villager reported that with each step, the orphan shone brighter with the confidence of one destined for royalty.

After the priest's final blessing, the prince called his guards to him.
"I must meet that young woman with the wreath. Ask her to come to me."

Thinking only of her mother's instructions to return home
immediately, the orphan had already fled into the square.

Swallowed up by the crowd, she grabbed a handful of coins from her pocket and threw them. The villagers scattered this way and that in reaching for the gold, and the orphan was able to make her escape. The guards were not fast enough to catch her.

Once home, the orphan sent the horse back into the sky, closed up all her gifts in the trunk, and took her place in the darkest corner of the cottage.

When the stepmother and her daughters returned, they could talk of nothing but the stranger who had enchanted all at church.

The orphan said not a word.

Meanwhile, no one could console the prince. He decided to return to the village church the next Sunday and find the beautiful stranger. As the day approached, he said to his guards, "Go to the palace beekeeper and have him prepare a mixture of honey and wax. Just before the service ends, spread a layer of it over the church threshold."

Once again the stepmother and her daughters fussed over their preparations for Sunday. Gowns were made, jewels were bought. And again, they commanded the orphan to fix their hair in towers of curls.

All happened as before. As soon as the stepmother and her sisters had left for church, the words of the orphan's mother came to her:

"Go, my child, go to good,
With all my blessings, go!…"

As before, the orphan bathed and combed her hair, then put on her gown, her glorious wreath, and her tiny shoes. Instantly, she became as brilliant as the sun, as beautiful as the moon, and as graceful as the dawn. She gathered a handful of gold coins and dropped them in her pocket.

Again, as the orphan rode to church on her radiant white mare, her mother's voice whispered through the trees:

"You must remember, my soul,
to return home the minute the service ends,
or all will be lost."

The orphan walked nobly down the aisle of the church, and the villagers could not keep their eyes off her. But no one was more captivated than the prince himself.

When the service was
almost over, the guards went to work pouring
the mixture of honey and wax across the church's
threshold. As soon as the priest said "Amen," the orphan
dashed from her seat and ran toward the door. Reaching the
threshold before any of the villagers, she stepped into the honey
and wax, and her feet stuck fast.

With all her might, she forced herself forward . . .

. . . leaving one of her shoes behind in the sticky trap.

As the prince's guards closed in, the orphan tossed her coins into the crowd. The villagers scattered, and she made her escape.

She mounted her mare and galloped away, leaving the guards empty-handed.

What should they do?

What *could* they do?

Why, they dragged themselves to the prince with the bad news, of course. "The maiden with the wreath is too clever for us," they declared. "Just when we thought we had her, she vanished into thin air. All we could capture of her was this shoe."

But out of the prince's disappointment, another plan took shape. "Go to the village," he told his guards. "Let it be known that every maiden, rich and poor, must come to the palace to try on this shoe. The one whose foot can fit inside will be my bride."

And so it happened that from dawn to dusk and dusk to dawn, day after day, maiden after maiden, foot after foot, and groan after groan, candidates came and tried on the shoe . . . but nothing.

Meanwhile, the stepsisters spent hour after hour and day after day fretting over what they would wear to see the prince. At last, as dusk fell on the third day, they hastened to the palace to try their luck. And was the orphan with them? Of course not.

Left alone, once again the girl heard her mother's voice:

"Go, my child, go to good,
With all my blessings, go!..."

Not a minute did the girl waste. She ran to the trunk, flung it open, and took out Mother Nature's gifts. She bathed and dressed, becoming as brilliant as the sun, as beautiful as the moon, as graceful as the dawn. But this time, instead of taking the gold coins, she found the jewels her stepmother and sisters had worn to the first church service and put them in her pocket.

Outside, the orphan reached for a passing cloud and, like that, the white mare appeared before her. As quick as the wind, she rode to the palace.

So radiant was she when she entered the great hall that everyone stopped to stare.

The prince stood enraptured. He bowed to the beautiful stranger, knelt down, and offered her the shoe.

Did the shoe fit the orphan's tiny foot?

Yes, it did. Perfectly!

No words could
describe the happiness
of the prince and
the orphan.

When the orphan caught sight of her stepmother and sisters, she went
to them and handed them their jewels.

"*You* are the maiden with the wreath?" cried all three in a single
stunned voice. And in the next instant, they fled from the palace.

A few weeks later, the prince and the orphan married.
They say their wedding had no equal for happiness and grandeur.
I was there, I should know.